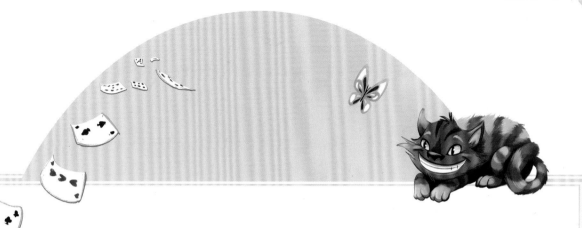

This igloo book belongs to:

....

igloobooks

Published in 2019
by Igloo Books Ltd
Cottage Farm
Sywell
NN6 0BJ
www.igloobooks.com

Copyright © 2017 Igloo Books Ltd
Igloo Books is an imprint of Bonnier Books UK

1219 003
8 10 12 11 9 7
ISBN 978-1-78557-867-0

Based on the original story by Lewis Carroll
Illustrated by Eva Morales
Written by Jan Payne

Cover designed by Lee Italiano
Interiors designed by Justine Ablett
and Katie Messenger
Edited by Hannah Cather

Printed and manufactured in China

Alice in Wonderland

igloobooks

One sunny afternoon, Alice and her sister were sitting in the garden. Her sister had her nose in a book and Alice was bored. She was just about to begin making a daisy chain when a white rabbit, with pink eyes, ran past. **"I'm late! I'm late!"** cried the rabbit.

The rabbit scurried off across the lawn. **"Oh my ears and whiskers!"** he cried, diving down a round, dark hole.
"Wait for me," called Alice, running after him.
She peered down the hole and, before she knew it,
Alice felt herself falling. Down, down she went.

Alice landed with a **bump**!
She found herself in a room with a tiny
door, which led to a beautiful garden.
"I'm too big to get through," she thought.
Then, on a glass table, she saw a golden
key and bottle with a label that said,
'drink me'.
"Curiouser and curiouser,"
whispered Alice. She took a
sip from the bottle.

Suddenly, she began to **shrink**.
Soon, Alice was no bigger than
the White Rabbit.

Alice went to open the door, but found she had left the key on the table.

drink me

She cried and cried and soon, Alice was floating in a pool of tears.

"Grab my tail," called a mouse as he swam towards her. The mouse towed Alice to a safe place on the shore.

After a while, Alice heard the pattering of footsteps as the White Rabbit ran up to her. **"My goodness! I'm late! Oh my fur and whiskers!"** Thinking Alice was his maid, he told her to go into his house and fetch his gloves and fan.

So, Alice went inside the rabbit's house.

Inside the cottage, a table was laid with scrumptious things to eat, including a chocolate cake with the words 'eat me' on it in icing. Alice cut a piece and took a large bite.

Suddenly, she felt herself getting **taller** and **taller** and **taller**, until, with a bump, her head hit the ceiling.

The White Rabbit was cross.
"I have an appointment with the Queen," he said, **"and you are blocking the door."**

Alice sobbed and, without thinking, fanned herself with the White Rabbit's magic fan. Immediately, she began to shrink. **"Will I ever be my right size again?"** she wailed.

Alice left the Rabbit's house and walked on. Soon, she heard a sleepy voice, but saw no one, only a mushroom that was about her size. Stretching on tiptoe, Alice peered over the edge and saw a large, blue caterpillar, smoking a strange pipe.

"If you eat two pieces of my special mushroom, one will make you bigger and one will make you smaller," said the Caterpillar.

So, Alice ate one piece of the mushroom and saved the second piece for later. Instantly, Alice began to grOW. Soon, she was her normal size again.

"I really must go and try to get into the garden," said Alice.

In the woods, Alice was startled to find a cat that grinned from ear to ear.
"I'm the Cheshire Cat," he said, grinning at her from a branch.
"Cheshire Cat, which way should I go from here?" asked Alice.

"The March Hare's house is that way," said the cat.
"Are you playing croquet with the Queen today?"

"I haven't been invited," replied Alice, but the cat just smiled and slowly disappeared.

Alice followed the Cheshire Cat's directions until she came to a pretty garden, where the March Hare and the Hatter were taking tea under a tree. Sitting between them, fast asleep, was a dormouse.

"No room!" they cried out, huddling together, when they saw Alice.

"There's plenty of room," said Alice, crossly, and sat down.

The Hatter opened his eye wide and looked at Alice.
"Why is a raven like a writing desk?" he asked her.
Alice thought and thought about ravens and desks.
"I give up," she said after quite some time.
"What's the answer?"
"I haven't the slightest idea," the Hatter replied.

Alice was very confused so she got up and walked off.
"I'll never come here again," she huffed.
"This is the stupidest tea party I've ever been to."

Alice left the garden and walked back to the woods. She found a door that led back to the glass table with the golden key. Nibbling the second piece of the Caterpillar's mushroom, Alice shrank. Soon, she was small enough to fit through the tiny door and enter the little garden.

There, she found pretty heart-shaped trees and brightly coloured flowers.

Suddenly, a procession came towards Alice and there were shouts of, **"The Queen! The Queen!"** Alice saw the White Rabbit, the Knave of Hearts and then the King and Queen of Hearts.

"Who are you?" asked the Queen.

"Alice, Your Majesty," replied the girl.
"You shall play croquet," commanded the Queen.

Alice thought she had never seen such a curious croquet ground in her life. The croquet balls were live hedgehogs and the mallets, live flamingos.

The card soldiers had to use their hands and feet to make the arches.

The players all played at once, without waiting for turns, quarrelling all the while and fighting for the hedgehogs.

In a very short time, the Queen was in a furious temper and went stamping about and shouting, **"Off with his head!"** about once a minute.

Alice was looking around for some way of escape, when she noticed the Cheshire Cat had appeared.

"How are you getting on?" asked the cat.

"I don't think they play at all fairly," Alice said, in a rather complaining tone. "And all they do is quarrel."

"How do you like the Queen?" asked the Cheshire Cat, in a whisper.

"Not at all," replied Alice.

Suddenly, someone yelled, **"The trial's started!"**

In a courtroom, the Knave of Hearts stood before the King and Queen. The White Rabbit began to speak...

"The Queen of Hearts,
she made some tarts,
all on a summer's day.
The Knave of Hearts,
he stole those tarts
and took them quite away!"

"Call the witness!"
cried the King.

As Alice took to the witness stand, she had the curious feeling that she was starting to grOW!

"What do you know about this business?" the King asked Alice.

"Nothing whatsoever," replied Alice.

The King asked the jury to consider their verdict.

"No, no! Sentence first, verdict after!" cried the Queen.

"Stuff and nonsense!" said Alice, loudly.

"The idea of having the sentence before the verdict!"

"Off with her head!" screamed the Queen.

By now, Alice was almost her full size.
"Who cares for you?" she shouted.
"You're nothing but a pack of cards!"

At this, the whole pack rose up and came flying down upon Alice. The cards were soon spinning all around her, so Alice closed her eyes and wished them away.

Suddenly, Alice found herself lying on a bank in the garden. Her head was in the lap of her sister, who was gently brushing away some dead leaves that had fluttered down from the trees upon her face. **"Wake up, Alice dear,"** said her sister. Alice smiled and thought what a wonderful dream it had been.